The Mystery Squad and the Candid Camera

Martin Waddell

Illustrated by Terry McKenna

Blackie

British Library Cataloguing in Publication Data
Waddell, Martin
The mystery squad and the candid camera
I. Title
823'.914 [J]   PZ7

ISBN 0-216-91711-5
ISBN 0-216-91710-7 Pbk

The Blackie Publishing Group
Furnival House, 14/18 High Holborn
London WC1V 6BX

Printed in Great Britain by
Thomson Litho Limited, East Kilbride, Scotland

Are You a Good Detective?

To solve this case you have to follow the trail wherever it leads you and spot the clues on the way. Some are in the story, some are in the pictures. If you crack the clues first time you get maximum points and end up with a Sherlock Holmes Detective Rating. If you don't, you may find further clues to help you but Beware of Custard Pies!

Add up your points as you go along and check your score against the Detective Rating Chart on page 96. You'll find out how good you really are!

A book for

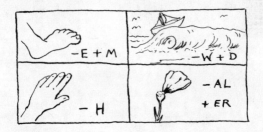

If you can't decode this, turn to **21**.
No detective rating points. This is just for code-breaking practice!

The Mystery begins here . . .

1

'Holiday jobs!' moaned James.

'When I grow up I'm going to be a rich gangster. Then I won't have to do any work!' I said.

That's the trouble about having parents like ours who run a cafe . . . you get left with all the cleaning up to do!

'*If* you grow up,' said Beans, between balloon puffs. 'You won't if you drop any more stuff!'

1

It wasn't my fault about the frying fat on the floor. I didn't *mean* it to get there, I didn't mean Dad to slip and anyway he shouldn't have been carrying so many eggs at one time.

'Anyone fancy an omelette for supper?' Beans said, grinning.

'What are *you* doing anyway?' I demanded.

'Bacon Balloonograms!' said Beans.

'Eh?' said James, swinging round from the window.

'You're not the only one in the Mystery Squad who can come up with inventions, James!' Beans said, and she showed us how a Balloonogram works.

'Then you can make the message re-appear by blowing the balloon up again?' said James.

'Right!' said Beans. 'The Bacon Balloonogram patented by B. Bacon for use in Mystery Squad Special Operations!'

James is the one who usually comes up with Mystery Squad inventions.

Beans normally specialises in codes. I am in charge of Mystery Squad TSM (Top Secret Material) which means I keep records of all our cases and the methods we use detecting things. Casey Peters is the Leader of the Mystery Squad, and the only one in it who isn't a Bacon. We let him be leader because his dad is a policeman. Casey is a brilliant detective.

The brilliant detective chose that moment to arrive, skidding up the pavement on his bike and almost crashing through our front window.

'Hey!' James said, pulling open the door.

'That lorry!' Casey panted.

1

'He nearly hit me!' Casey said. 'He pulled out from the kerb, without any signal!'

'You've banjaxed your front light!' James said, picking the bicycle up.

'Oh great! Super!' Casey said, sounding really cross. 'That's all I needed! Some noodle of a lorry driver making me crash!'

'Anybody get the lorry number?' said Beans.

Observation Test!

Did you get the number of the lorry?
No turning back to check!
If you think it was . . .

OBH 239K turn to section **82**.

OHG 339R turn to section **47**.

OBJ 393Y turn to section **26**.

KLM 239M turn to section **19**.

NOK 391L turn to section **33**.

2

Wrong! Go to **56** and try again.

3

Right! What's the point of doing it, though? If you think it is . . .

Safety in numbers, turn to **60**.

To give you a chance to get to Casey's dad, turn to **73**.

To give you a chance to establish who is following you, turn to **81**.

All these things, turn to **63**.

4

But the police *were* confused! Go to **40** and try again.

5

There is no evidence to suggest that either Harry Roy or Derek Burn were involved . . . *yet*. Go to **70** and think again.

6

Detective Rating

6 points if you got it.

Deduct 1 point for each mistake you made. More than six mistakes, 0 points!

1 bonus point for knowing why!

6

'If Smithson and Paul Gemini are in it together, they don't need someone else disguised as Paul Gemini, do they? But we *know* there *is* someone disguised as Paul Gemini, because Bodger bumped into him, remember? So did I . . . at a time when the *real* Paul Gemini was being interviewed by your dad, Casey, down at the police station!'

There was a long silence when Beans finished.

'Pity about that!' said Casey.

'It was a good theory,' James admitted. 'But now we're back where we began! Not Who-Dunnit, but How-Was-It-Done!'

'And Two Paul Geminis to account for,' said Beans.

'Plus one black wig,' said James.

Casey brightened up.

'Two wigs, probably,' he said. 'A black wig to hide a red wig!'

'Eh?' said James.

'The person who was disguised as Paul Gemini must have worn a red wig,' said Casey. 'A Paul Gemini disguise wouldn't work without one. But a head of red hair like that is the sort of thing someone might remember . . . so the fake Paul Gemini wore a black wig to cover the red wig, *except* when he was pretending to be Paul Gemini for the benefit of the camera in Smithson's office.'

'That doesn't *sound* right to me,' said Beans.

Nobody else said anything.

We were all too muddled up with fake Paul Geminis and real Paul Geminis and black wigs and red wigs and fingerprints and alibis.

'This is all *theories*!' said James.

'We've got *my* information,' said Beans.

'What information?' said James.

'The house,' Beans said. 'I know where the fake Paul Gemini lives, because I spotted him there, keeping an eye on you lot when you were in the Omega scrap yard.'

'Third house on the right!' said Casey.

'All we have to do is to tell your dad that the fake Paul Gemini lives there and then the police can go round and arrest him!' said Beans.

'Y-e-s,' said Casey, uncomfortably.

'But you're afraid to do it!' said Beans.

'Everything we've told Dad so far has ended up making us look silly,' said Casey.

'We weren't silly, though,' James objected. 'Bodge's cold chips question was a sensible one, and

Beans did see the fake Paul Gemini going into the scrap yard, heading for the Mini . . . '

'From which he has probably moved the money, by now!' Beans grumbled. 'He had it hidden where he could keep an eye on it, right opposite his front door!'

'We ought to try talking to your dad again, Casey,' said James.

'You do it!' said Casey.

James didn't fancy it!

Nobody did! Casey's dad is almost impossible to talk to when he is busy and we'd already had two goes at telling him things, which hadn't worked out.

'We have to be sure of our facts this time,' said James. 'We can't risk being wrong again. Suppose Beans got the wrong house . . . '

'I didn't!' said Beans, indignantly.

'I want to do *something*!' I said. 'If we don't do something soon, it will be too late!'

'Yes, but what?' said James.

As usual, it was Casey who knew what to do.

'The fake Paul Gemini has been using the house to keep an eye on the scrap yard,' he said. 'Suppose we reverse the operation. We set up surveillance on the house, using the scrap yard.'

'Great hiding places!' said Beans.

'We reckon he's got the money,' said Casey. 'Either he has it in the house, or it is hidden somewhere else. Sooner or later he will have to move it. We wait, and watch, and when he comes out with the money, or goes out to collect it from wherever it is hidden now, we tail him . . . if we can tell Dad where the money is, he'll have to take notice!'

That's what we did.

We set up our surveillance posts in the scrap yard. Bet you can't spot us!

Then suddenly Casey's dad appeared at the gate.

'Dad!' Casey called. 'Dad!'

His dad jumped! He'd come to check the Mini and he hadn't spotted us.

'What are you lot doing here?' he spluttered.

'Keeping surveillance on the fake Paul Gemini's house!' Beans said. 'I spotted it. It's the third house on the right, as you go out of the gate.'

'What are you kids on about? That's the *real* Paul Gemini's house,' said Casey's dad.

We told him everything, several times!

This time, he listened.

'The fake one and the real one must be in it together, Dad!' Casey said. 'The fake Paul Gemini did the robbery and the real one provided him with all the information. They used the Paul Gemini disguise to provide a cast iron alibi for the real Paul Gemini.'

'Two Paul Geminis?' Casey's dad said. 'Both using the same house? Are you kids dead sure of your facts?'

'I am sure that I saw the fake one, in that house, while the real one was in your office, Mr Peters,' Beans said. 'Cross my heart and knit my fingers!'

'Two Geminis!' said Casey's dad.

'Oh no!' Casey exclaimed, suddenly. 'Gemini. G-E-M-I-N-I! Gemini, Dad!'

'Eh?' said Mr Peters.

'G-E-M-I-N-I!' moaned Casey. 'It isn't a *real* name . . . they're playing clever clogs with us, the two of them! Once you get the *Gemini* bit, everything else makes sense! Even the rotten wig . . . it wasn't a black wig to cover a red wig . . .

'You said it was!' I objected.

'It wasn't . . . not with *Gemini* in the case,' said Casey. 'It was a black *wig* to cover red *hair*!'

We all thought he'd gone bonkers!

'A black wig to cover red hair?' muttered James.

'Two redheads!' said Casey. 'G-E-M-I-N-I. Don't you get it?'

Do you get it?

If you get it, move to **13**.

If you need a clue, turn to **34**.

7

Detective Rating

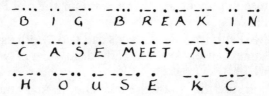

3 points if you got the message right.

Deduct 1 point for each word you got wrong, and 1 point if you needed help. With 3 or more points deducted, you score 0.

7

'You got here!' Casey said. 'Took you long enough!'

He was leaning against the door of his garage. We use Casey's garage to hold Mystery Squad Meetings about our cases and to do some other things as well. They are TSM and I am not at liberty to divulge what they are but we couldn't do them that morning because we hadn't got the time or the sausages!

'What's the Big Break then?' said James. 'What's so important that you couldn't put it in a note?'

'This is,' said Casey, and he held out a photograph to us.

'It's the Mystery Man!' Beans gasped. 'He's a safebreaker!'

'Caught in the act!' I said.

'Photographed in the act,' said Casey. 'The criminal in this picture apparently didn't realise that the office had a remote control security camera in it!'

'Where is this?' James said.

'The Star Cinema, down in the town centre,' said Casey. 'The office was broken into yesterday and the day's takings were removed from the safe.'

'By our Mystery Man!' said Beans.

'He must have had an accomplice who drove the getaway lorry. The accomplice hit him over the head and took all the money and now our Mystery Man is pretending to have amnesia because he *can't* tell the police what happened!' I said.

Casey grinned.

'James?' he said.

'Our Mystery Man didn't pull the Star Cinema job,' said James. 'The picture proves that, conclusively!'

Conclusive proof?

If you know what the proof is, turn to **70**.

If you need a clue, turn to **49**.

8

Wrong! Go to **45** covered in pie crust!

9

Irrelevant! Go to **56**.

10

A gluggy custard pie for guessing! Go to **63** and try again.

11

First word of message: B I G

Now go to **55** and tackle the rest of the message.

12

Detective Rating

4 points if you got it.

Deduct 1 point for each mistake you made.

Score 0 points if you got custard-pied!

12

'The man who used this wig *hasn't* got black hair!' said Casey. 'If he had, he wouldn't need a black wig, would he?'

'Great!' I said.

'True, as far as it goes,' said James.

'It might go quite a long way,' said Casey, with a frown. 'This case obviously involves people using disguises, though we can't work out how. Now at least we know something about one of them.'

'That he wanted to be mistaken for someone with black hair?' said James. 'Who?'

'Derek Burn at the cinema has black hair,' said Casey. 'Harry Roy hasn't any hair, and Smithson is sort of mousey.'

'None of them look like Paul Gemini,' I said.

'Not so's you'd notice,' said Casey.

'Maybe we're not *supposed* to notice,' said James. 'If we're talking about an expert in disguises, the baldness could be fake, couldn't it?'

'Fat old Harry Roy could be young and slim!' I said. 'The Mystery of the Master Disguiser!'

'What now?' said James.

'Nothing for it but to tell Dad about the Mini, and show him the wig,' said Casey.

We started for the gate, but we didn't get far.
A little kid came up on a tricycle.
'You Casey Peters?' he said.
'Yes.'
'Girl gave me this for you,' he said, and rode off.
Casey opened the piece of paper.

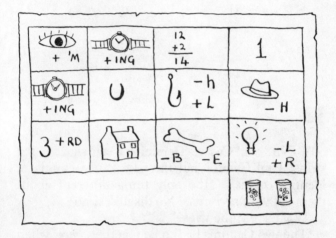

'It's a message from Beans!' he said. 'That's her sign at the end!'

Beans always uses a tin of Beans as her sign in code messages. We started working out the rest of the message.

Can you read Beans's message?

If you can, turn to **25**.

If you need help with the first line turn to **50**.

If you need help with the second line turn to **69**.

If you need help with the third line turn to **62**.

Detective Rating

6 points if you realised the truth straight away.

5 points if you needed one clue, 3 points if you needed two clues, and 1 point if you had to decode it!

13

'TWINS!' said Casey. 'Gemini is a star sign . . . the twins! Paul Gemini and the fake Paul Gemini are identical twins . . . the only thing different about them is their *fingerprints*! No disguises, no . . . '

'What about the wigs?'

'The two Geminis had to be together, *once*, when Paul was being driven to the place where he was dumped, in the alley behind our shop,' Casey said. 'Two identical redheads, in the lorry. Somebody might have spotted them together, and remembered. So one of them wore the black wig!'

'Then the second twin drove back to the cinema, did the job, and took the money off in the van . . . '

'Leaving his twin with a perfect alibi!'

'Only because I found him in time!' I objected.

'If you hadn't found the twin in the alley, he would have recovered, and made sure he was discovered,' said Casey. 'His feet were loosely bound.

I wondered about that . . . and about the footprints by the puddle . . . '

'Only going in one direction?' James said. Trust James to spot it.

'Yes,' said Casey. 'It could have meant that Paul Gemini was carried up the alley and dumped by someone who managed to walk back without making any footprints, or that Paul Gemini *walked* up the alley by himself!'

'Why did they have to make it all so complicated?' I said.

'Because of the camera in the cinema office,' said James. 'They knew they would be filmed. The only way to beat the camera was to have a cast iron alibi.'

'They used the camera to lie for them!' said Casey. 'They staged their own Candid Camera act, showing the fingerprints being planted. But the fingerprints didn't match Paul Gemini's. No wonder! They belonged to his twin.'

'What happens now?' I said.

We all looked at Casey's dad.

'Aren't you going to arrest Paul Gemini?' I said.

'No,' he said.

'NO?'

'I want to get both of them,' Casey's dad said. 'Both of them, *and the money*!'

'And if we move in and arrest the twin who is in the house, we may scare the other one into running?' said Casey.

'Right!' said his dad.

Then he went to the scrap man's hut, and started making his arrangements, barking orders down his two-way radio. The house had to be surrounded, without the Paul Gemini who was inside knowing what was going on, and without the other twin being able to spot what was happening, if he came back.

This is Casey's dad's plan.

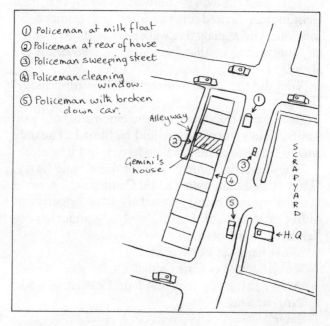

① Policeman at milk float
② Policeman at rear of house
③ Policeman sweeping street
④ Policeman cleaning window.
⑤ Policeman with broken down car.

Alleyway

Gemini's house

SCRAPYARD

← H.Q

'All points covered,' said Casey's dad. 'Now we wait.'

We waited.

And waited.

And waited.

'When's something going to happen?' Beans moaned.

'Whenever Gemini Number Two returns!' said Casey.

'Suppose he's in there already?' said Beans.

'Dad?' said Casey.

His dad turned away from watching Gemini Number One, who was casually reading his paper by the window of the house, where he could see out over the scrap yard.

'What, Casey?' he said.

'Suppose they are *both* in there, Dad?' said Casey.

'If they are, we'll know about it soon enough,' said Casey's dad.

'How?' said Casey.

'Oldest trick in the book, son. Why do you think I've got one of my men in the back entry, where he can't see anything?'

'In case they attempt to escape round the back?' Casey said.

'Nope!' said Casey's dad. 'There's a police car at the end of the entry, they can't get out. The man in the entry isn't there to stop them. He's there to listen!'

'What for?' said James.

'*Water*,' said Mr Peters.

We all looked blank.

'Gemini Number One is at the window, keeping an eye out for trouble,' said Mr Peters. 'If Gemini Number Two is in there, sooner or later he'll give himself away.'

'Oh,' said Casey. 'GOT IT!'

'Thought you would!' said his dad.

Do you get it?

If you understand move to **64**.

If you must have a clue, go to **83**.

14

Detective Rating

3 points if you realised that Casey wanted to photograph the footprints by the puddle, plus 1 bonus point if you worked out that the footprints had to be photographed before the rain washed them away.

Deduct 1 point for each wrong choice you made but score 0 points if you got custard pied!

14

The ambulance pulled away, with the Mystery Man inside.

Casey's dad came back into the shop, and started asking questions. We told him what we knew, and then Casey showed him the photographs.

'Not bad, Casey,' said his dad. 'But . . . '

'I know, Dad,' said Casey. 'I'm sorry!'

I looked at Beans. I couldn't figure out what he was sorry about. We'd managed to photograph the footprints before the rain washed them away, which I reckoned was pretty good.

What had Casey done wrong?

If you think he had . . .

Disturbed the scene of the crime turn to **67**.

Photographed the wrong thing turn to **75**.

Forgotten to wait for the police before doing anything turn to **44**.

Forgotten something else turn to **51**.

Detective Rating

2 points if you spotted that the wrecked car had been removed from the lorry.

Deduct 1 point if you needed help.

15

'The car!' said Beans. 'There was an old beaten up car on the back of the lorry, and it has been dumped. Right?'

'Right!' said Casey.

'What *sort* of car?' said James.

Nobody was very sure, until I got out my car profiles. I have special files of shapes in my TSM notebook and car profiles is one of them.

'I reckon it's one of these,' I said.

Which one?

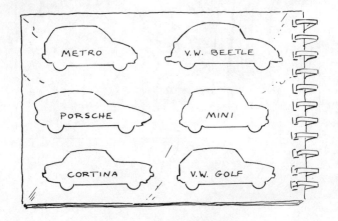

Pick the type of car on the back of the lorry by going through these profiles . . . You'll score extra if you don't have to look at the pictures in **1**.

Go to **76**.

16

Smithson could be lying, no proof one way or the other! Go to **56**.

17

Here's your clue. Go to **15**.

18

But Smithson evidently *was* deceived! Go to **40** and think again.

19

This is nothing like the number! Go to **1** and try again.

20

Wrong! Go to **45** and reconsider.

21

A book for

= toe − E = to + M = TOM

= wave − W = ave + D = DAVE

= hand − H = AND

= petal − AL = pet + ER = Peter

= A book for TOM DAVE AND PETER . . .
Now go to section 1 and get on with it!

22

Right! But *who?* Go to **77** when you've worked it out.

23

Wrong! If the real Paul Gemini was attacked after he bought the chips, the chips must have taken at least twenty minutes to reach Mr Smithson . . . cold chips! Go to **70** and think again.

24

Doesn't prove anything! Go to **56** and try again.

Detective Rating

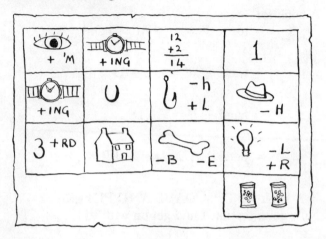

2 points for each line in the message that you got right.
0 points for any line you needed help with.

25

I'M WATCHING SOMEONE
WATCHING YOU LOOK AT
THIRD HOUSE ON RIGHT

'Third house on the right?' said Casey.

'*Don't* look, Bodge!' said James, urgently.

'But the note says . . . '

'I don't care what the note says,' said James. 'If
you look, you let the person who is watching us know

that we *know* we're being watched, don't you? So long as he or she doesn't know, we have the advantage!'

'What do we do then?' I said.

What would you do?

Make a run for it, keeping together? Turn to **65**.

Split up, and make a run for it in different directions? Turn to **43**.

Stay where you are? Turn to **48**.

Walk slowly back to Casey's house, keeping together? Turn to **3**.

Detective Rating

3 points for OBJ 393Y first time.
Deduct 1 point for each mistake you made.
2 or more mistakes, 0 points!

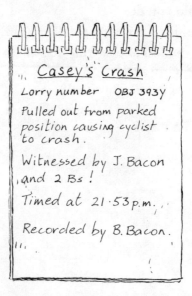

26

'I got it all down in my TSM book!' I said.

'Great!' said Casey.

'Looks like you've been useful for once,' said Beans.

'But inaccurate!' said James.

'Eh?'

'It says *Witnessed by J. Bacon and Two Bs*,' said James. 'I'm J. Bacon and I didn't witness it. I was mucking about with balloons. So were you two!'

'We *heard* it!' said Beans.

'You heard Casey crashing into the window!' said James. 'Then you heard what he *said* had happened . . . that is all you are a witness to. Right, Casey?'

'Right,' said Casey. 'Inaccurate entry! Be more careful next time, Bodge!' Then he looked gloomy. 'No witnesses! Just my word against the driver!'

'Tough!' said James.

I left them moaning about it!

I was fed up anyway. It was B. Bacon the Brilliant who had got the Vital Evidence down, while everybody else was picking Casey up and examining his bicycle. I reckoned James was getting at me again.

'Is anybody going to help with these bins?' I said.

'I'm blowing up balloons,' said Beans.

'And we're watching her,' said James and Casey.

'Oh great!' I said. 'Brilliant! Thanks a lot!'

'When you grow up you can be a bin-man,' said Beans, between puffs. 'It would suit you better than being a gangster.'

'Bacon's Bins!' said Casey.

'Bin-bungling our speciality!' said Beans. 'Have your bins bungled by Bacon! Guaranteed rubbish everywhere!' Then she started to tell Casey about the eggs.

The way she told it, Dad was covered in egg from head to toe.

'Stop exaggerating!' I said.

'No *Egg*-xaggeration!' Beans said. 'The yolk's on you, Bodge!'

'On Dad, you mean,' said James. 'He was yolked all over.'

I went out with the bin to the alley, remembering
to step round the slippy bit where Dad did his egg-
dive.

Then . . .

'Don't move him!' James said. 'Something might be broken!' We untied the gag from the man's mouth, and the rope from round his arms.

'Uh . . . aaah!' the man said, clutching his head. He had red hair, which was wet and bedraggled from the rain.

He tried to get up, and I took his arm.

'Careful!' James said.

'S'right!' the man said, shakily. 'I'm a'right. I'm . . . where am I?'

'Take it easy,' James said.

'I . . . I . . .' the man stuttered. 'Who . . . where . . . what happened?'

We helped him into the house. Then my dad came and he rang for the ambulance and the police.

'Doesn't know where he is, who he is, or how he got there!' I told Casey, who had gone out again to the back alley, to mark out the spot where we'd found the man.

'We need a camera, Bodge,' Casey said. 'Quickly!'

'What for?' I said.

What does Casey want to photograph?

If you think it is . . .

turn to **80**.

turn to **68**.

turn to **61**.

turn to **46**.

27   − · · · · · − − ·

That is your clue . . . but you'll have to decode it, using the Morse code shown in **55**. Move to **70** when you've worked out what it means. If you can't work it out, go to **70** anyway!

28

This fits with the idea that Gemini and Smithson set up the job together! It doesn't disprove anything! Go to **56** and think again.

29

Wrong. Paul Gemini turned up among the bins, at least ten minutes away from the Star Cinema, at 21.50 approx. Ten minutes there, ten minutes back again . . . the chips *must* have been cold . . . and then you have to add in the time for the attack on Paul Gemini. Go to **70** and think again.

30

Wrong! We're talking about a criminal. He could have stolen the black wig! Go to **45** and reconsider.

31

Here's a pie-full for guessing! Go to **63** and try again.

32

Check the picture in **7**. Think about the desk. Got it?
Turn to **40**.

If you need another clue, turn to **52**.

33

Wrong. Go to **1** and try again.

34

That is your clue. If you get it, go to **13**.
If you need a second clue, turn to **42**.

35

Detective Rating

6 points if you spotted that Smithson must be lying if he said the chips were hot!

Deduct 2 points for each wrong choice you made.

Score 0 points if you got custard pied!

35

'If the man who attacked Paul Gemini also delivered the chips, the chips must have been cold,' said Casey. 'Either that, or there were no chips! If Smithson said they were hot, he has to be lying.'

'But they fought about them!' said Beans, mystified. 'The fake Paul Gemini brought Smithson plaice, instead of cod . . . '

'Smithson *says*,' said Casey.

All the Bacons looked bewildered.

'Why would he lie about that?' James said, and then. 'Oh! Gotcha!'

'A frame-up,' said Casey. 'The idea was to knock Gemini over the head, dump him in an alley to sleep it off, and stage the robbery using someone dressed as Gemini. When the police came looking, Gemini would have no alibi.'

'He has an alibi!' Beans broke in. 'We're it!'

'We are,' said James. 'We are because we found him in time. If we'd found him an hour and a half later, no-one would have believed that he hadn't set it up to account for the time when the crime was being committed. Gemini would have tried to explain that he was lying in our entry . . . when all the time the hidden camera in the Manager's office was filming the fake Paul Gemini committing the crime! No-one would have believed his story!'

'The Hot Chip Hoax!' I said. 'Or the Cold Chip Caper! Which do you like best?'

'Hadn't we better find out what Smithson *said* about the chips first?' said James. 'We're building great theories about the chips being hot . . . supposing he said they were cold? Then the evidence that Smithson was lying is non-existent.'

'Y-e-s,' said Casey. 'But . . . '

'But what?' said James.

'The idea of a frame-up isn't,' said Casey. 'The police would never have believed Paul Gemini's story of being knocked out and dumped in the alley. Somebody set out to frame him, someone who knew there was a camera in the office, someone who knew all about the safe, someone who knew when Paul Gemini would go to buy chips, and where he would go . . . '

'One of the cinema staff!' said Beans.
I wrote the names down in my TSM notebook.

"SMITHSON... manager...
hot / cold chips?

Mrs. Patrick ... ticket lady
... did she leave at 21-45?

Derek Burn... usher...
chip buyer?

Harry Roy... usher...
chip buyer?

'Four suspects to begin with,' James said, 'and not much to go on. We'd better check this chip thing first . . .'
'How?' said Beans.
'I'm not asking your dad, Casey!' I said, hurriedly.
'Neither am I,' said Casey.
'In that case, we fall back on routine,' said James. 'My department, I think. Map, Bodge?'
I got him a map out of our files, showing the Star Cinema, and the streets around it. James started drawing circles on it, using the Star Cinema as the centre.

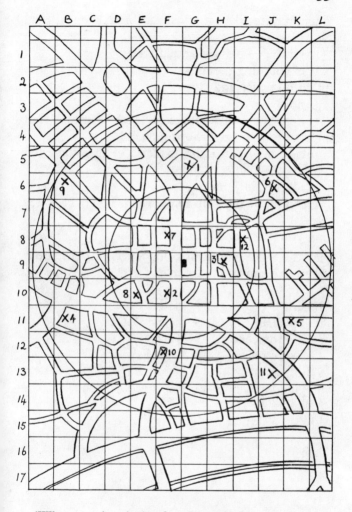

'What are the circles for, James?' Beans asked.
'Time,' said James. 'The first circle shows places
which are within five minutes of the Star, the second

is ten minutes. I've marked each chip shop with an X . . .'

'And the take-aways?' said Casey.

'I'm counting them,' said James. 'Anywhere that might do plaice and chips!'

'And?'

'There are twelve altogether,' said James. 'That means we visit three shops each.'

'Make a map-reading exercise of it,' suggested Casey.

'Right!' said James.

He gave me my map references: G.5, B.11, J.13.

Can you map read?

Pick the three chip shops Bodger had to visit from the twelve shown on the map.

1 Bird's	7 the Kentucky
2 Hawaiian Fry	8 the Sky Blue
3 El Tropicano	9 Westys
4 the Titanic	10 Fry's Fry
5 Bob's Fry	11 El Munchoe
6 Kingdom's	12 Neptune's House

Move to **57** when you've done it.

36

Here's a fat bald custard pie! Go to **63** and try again.

37

Hunt the Tiger! That's the clue.
Check the picture in **76**. Move to **45** when you've got it!

38

Not bad . . . but Smithson *could* have driven Paul Gemini to the entry. Go to **56**.

39

No evidence about this at all! You're custarded! Go to **45** and reconsider.

Detective Rating

*3 points if you spotted that the fake Paul Gemini had
removed his gloves before working on the safe.*

Deduct 1 point for each clue you needed.

40

'The fake Paul Gemini *took off* his gloves before he
worked on the safe!' said Casey.

'Fingerprints?' said James, waking up.

'Right,' said Casey. 'Fingerprints all over the
show. That proves one thing. Whatever the purpose
of the Paul Gemini disguise, it wasn't to . . . '

It wasn't to what?

If you think it wasn't to . . .

Deceive Mr Smithson, turn to **18**.

Confuse the police, turn to **4**.

Incriminate Paul Gemini, turn to **56**.

41

We don't know when the lorry was returned to the scrap yard . . . Smithson could have done it. Turn to **56**.

42

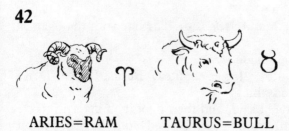

ARIES=RAM   TAURUS=BULL

That is your second clue. If you get it now, go to **13**. If you need a third clue, go to **54**.

43

Splitting up would ensure that two out of the three got away safely . . . but it is broad daylight, and there doesn't seem to be much danger. If there *is* any danger, one person on his own will be very much at risk! Splitting up isn't a great idea! Go to **25** and try again.

44

If Casey had waited for the police to come the evidence would have been wiped out. He had to act quickly. Go to **14**.

Detective Rating

3 points if you spotted the Mini.

Deduct 2 points if you needed a clue.

45

'There it is!' Casey said. 'The one with the tiger on it.'

We all made for it.

'Hold on!' James shouted. 'Beans! Bodge! Don't touch anything!'

'Why?' I said, and then I got it. 'Fingerprints?'

'Right,' said James. 'Nobody told the police about the Mini on the back of the lorry, so the chances are that they haven't been over it yet. If we go diving inside, we could mess the whole thing up.'

'I wonder how it got off the lorry?' Casey said, slowly.

'Somebody dumped it off, stupid!' said Beans.

'It's not as simple as that, Beans,' Casey said. 'According to my dad the Omega people didn't know that the lorry had left the scrap yard . . . '

'Doesn't say much for their security system!' James broke in.

'It is a scrap yard, not the Bank of England,' said Casey. 'People don't go pinching beaten up lorries to joyride in.'

'Somebody did!' I said.

'Right,' said Casey. 'Somebody took the lorry away, with the Mini that was on it. That makes sense. They wouldn't stand about taking the Mini off, if they were thinking of taking the lorry. The puzzling thing is what they did when they got back!'

'Unloaded the Mini?' said James. '*Right!*'

'Why?' said Casey. 'Why bring the lorry back here at all, for that matter? Why not just dump it somewhere, when the job was done?'

He waited for us to tell him. That's just like Casey. He had worked out some theory of his own, and he wanted to show off what a brilliant detective he was.

'Why use a scrap lorry at all?' he said. 'And why pick one with an old Mini loaded on it?'

'I know!' said Beans. 'You gave us tips on trailing people. One of the most important tips was always to be *doing* something, if you had to hang around waiting for somebody to show up. Standing watching makes people suspicious. Somebody doing a job is just that . . . somebody doing a job . . . no reason for anyone to suspect anything. So the man who took the lorry wanted to look as if he was out removing a broken-down Mini. He probably parked near the Star Cinema and pretended to be fixing his load on, while he was waiting for Paul Gemini to come out for the chips.'

'Oh,' Casey said. 'Hadn't thought of that! My idea was more to do with the Mini. I'm thinking about the loot. We know a lot of money was taken from the Star Cinema, and it had to be hidden *somewhere*, so . . . '

'In the Mini!' I said.

'Then the thief hides the Mini, in a pile of old cars,' said James. 'Not bad. The scrap yard people are obviously pretty dozy. They might not get round to tackling the Mini for ages. The money could stay in the boot . . . '

'Or hidden under one of the seats!' I said.

'Somewhere in the car, anyway,' said Casey.

'Let's take a look!' said Beans, but James grabbed her before she could get in.

'Fingerprints!' he snapped.

'Oh! Sorry!' Beans said.

'If we can't get into the car, there isn't much we can do, is there?' said James. 'Except report it to your dad.'

'We can look,' said Casey.

We had a good look inside, through the windows. There wasn't any glass in them, so that made it simpler. Here is what we saw.

'Look, there, under the seat!' Beans said.

'Looks like a plastic bag,' I said.

'The money!' Beans said, bouncing about.

'Better go and tell your dad we've found it, Casey,' I said.

Casey looked at James. James shrugged.

'You reckon?' Casey said to me. 'Mucked up footprints, questions about cold chips, and now "Please Dad, we've found a plastic bag!"'

Casey was right. I didn't fancy bringing his dad out on a plastic bag chase.

'You tell him, Bodge,' said Beans.

'Why me?' I said, smelling a rat.

'Because nobody else wants to,' said Beans. 'Right?' she grinned at Casey and James.

'Right,' said James.

'We've got to tell him,' I said. 'We've found something, haven't we?'

'If we knew for sure that the money was in the bag . . . ' Casey said.

'We can't know, without looking!' said Beans.

'Wait! Wait! Wait! Wait!' said James, his face clearing.

'What? What? What? What?' said Casey, annoyed at being interrupted.

'The Bacon Spare Arm!' said James.

Casey's face fell. 'Not another of your daft inventions!' he said.

'Daft or not, it works!' said James.

'I'll get it!' I said, and I nipped off down the road.

This is the Bacon Spare Arm.

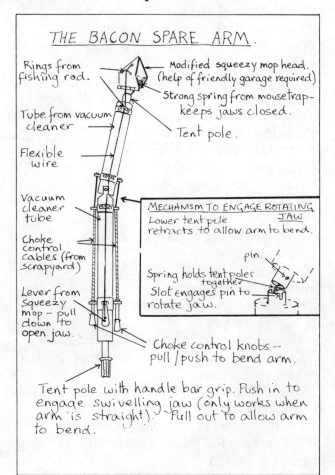

THE BACON SPARE ARM.

Rings from fishing rod.

Modified squeezy mop head. (help of friendly garage required)

Strong spring from mousetrap - keeps jaws closed.

Tube from vacuum cleaner

Tent pole.

Flexible wire

Vacuum cleaner tube

Choke control cables (from scrapyard)

Lever from squeezy mop — pull down to open jaw.

MECHANISM TO ENGAGE ROTATING JAW
Lower tent pole retracts to allow arm to bend.

pin.

Spring holds tent poles together
Slot engages pin to rotate jaw.

Choke control knobs — pull / push to bend arm.

Tent pole with handle bar grip. Push in to engage swivelling jaw (only works when arm is straight). Pull out to allow arm to bend.

James invented it for Mystery Squad Operations, but we also use it for doing the windows and things at home. I tried it fishing down a drain, but I didn't catch anything except a thumping from James.

It didn't take me long to get back home and pick up the Bacon Spare Arm from James's Den, and I was in full Bodger sprint on my way back when . . .

. . . I ran slam bam into Paul Gemini!

I reckon I nearly broke his leg, and he put a big bend in the Bacon Spare Arm when he landed on it.

Gemini was really mad!

He swore at me, and he called me names, and he made a real song and dance about it!

'You! Hey you! Who do you think you are! Dashing round like a runaway bullock! Rotten little tyke!'

'Sorry, Mr Gemini,' I said.

That stopped him.

He blinked at me.

'Don't you remember me?' I said.

'Oh,' he said. 'Oh yeah. Come down the Star, don't you?'

'Well . . . ' I said.

'You're one of those kids who sneak in the back, aren't you?' he said. 'I know you lot! Where do you live, anyway? What's your name? You've messed up my clothes good and proper . . . '

He advanced on me.

I didn't wait about.

'You hey you! Nipper!' I was off up the road.

He didn't bother coming after me, probably because he could see I was a Super-Fast Bodger Bacon Olympic sprinter, but more likely because he had somewhere else to go . . . like down to the police station for an interview with Casey's dad.

I told Casey all about it when I got back to the Omega scrap yard.

'Oh great!' Beans said. 'Now he'll go down to the cafe and complain to Dad and we'll all be in the soup.'

'He didn't recognise me,' I said. 'I almost saved his life last night, and he didn't recognise me this morning!'

'Just as well for you he didn't!' said James, and then we set about operating the Spare Arm.

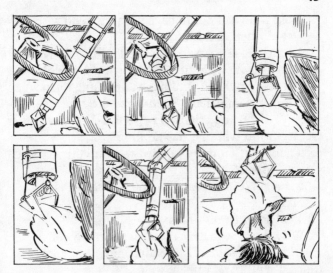

'A wig!" said James, looking at it.

'A *black* wig,' said Casey. 'I don't understand. Paul Gemini has *red* hair. If somebody wanted to dress up to impersonate him they would need a red wig, not a black one!'

'Joke!' Beans shouted. 'Joke! Joke!'

'Shut up, Beans,' said James.

'Doesn't anybody want to hear my joke?' said Beans.

'Only if you promise to shut up after telling it,' James said.

'Well,' said Beans. 'If it had been a *red* wig . . . if it *had* been . . . '

'It wasn't,' James objected.

'I know it wasn't, but *suppose* it had been, and

suppose it turned out to have nothing to do with the case at all then . . . then . . . '

'Don't crease yourself, Beans,' I said. 'You're ugly enough as it is, without a fold down the middle.'

'If it was a red wig, and if it had nothing to do with the case it would have been a red herring.' Beans said. 'R-E-D, red, right? H-A-I-R-I-N-G, hairing? Get it? A red wig that has nothing . . . '

'That's got nothing to do with anything!' said Casey, impatiently.

'It's a good joke though, isn't it?' said Beans.

'NO!'

'That's not funny, Beans!'

'Why don't you clear off with your silly jokes!'

'Okay!' she said. 'If nobody thinks my jokes are funny I will!' And off she went.

'Let her go!' James said. 'She wasn't helping anyway!'

'Not much to help with, is there?' I said, looking at the wig. 'A black wig doesn't tell us anything, does it?'

'It *has* to have something to do with the crime,' James said. 'We know this is the Mini that was on the lorry, and the black wig is hidden in it . . . somebody took care to hide it, where it wouldn't be found. There must be a reason for that!'

'It's not just an old joke shop cheap wig either,' I said. 'It's a good one.'

'It does tell us one thing about the person who used it,' said Casey, slowly.

'I don't think so,' said James.

What does the black wig tell you?

That the man who used it . . .

Was bald? Turn to **8**.

Had red hair? Turn to **20**.

Was rich? Turn to **30**.

Didn't have black hair? Turn to **12**.

Was one of the cinema staff (Roy/Burn/Smithson/ Mrs Patrick)? Turn to **39**.

46

These footprints were made by the Mystery Squad! They can photograph their own footprints any time. You are dripping custard pie! Go to **26** and think again.

47

You need your eyes tested! Go to **1** and try again.

48

For how long? The longer you stay, the more chance there is that the watcher will bring up reinforcements, and collar you! Go to **25** and think again.

49

Check Bodger's notebook entry about the lorry in **26**.

If you know how that helps, turn to **70**.

If you need another clue, turn to **27**.

50

$=$ I $+$ 'M $=$ *I'm*

$=$ watch $+$ ing $=$ *watching*

$$\begin{array}{r} 12 \\ +2 \\ \hline 14 \end{array} = \text{sum} = some$$

$=$ *one*

I'M WATCHING SOMEONE is the first line.
Go to **12**.

51

Right! But what did Casey forget to do? If you know, go to **55**. If you need a clue, turn to **58**.

52

What is lying *on* the desk and what has that got to do with Paul Gemini?

Try to work out what Casey has spotted, then turn to **40**.

53

Smithson could have done it, *after* the crime. Turn to **56** and think again.

54 $-$ $\cdot-\cdot$ $\cdot\cdot$ $-\cdot$ $\cdot\cdot\cdot$

Get the message?
Decode it, then go to **13**.

Detective Rating

*3 points if you realised that Casey should have put a
protective covering over the footprints, to prevent the rain
washing them out.*

1 point if you needed a clue.

*Deduct 1 point for each wrong choice you made. More
than three deductions — 0 points!*

55

It was dry the next morning, but James still wouldn't
give over about Casey forgetting to protect the
footprints from the rain!

'A bin-lid would have done,' said James. 'Anything like that! It really wasn't difficult!'

'*You* didn't do *anything*!' Beans pointed out, and
James almost choked over his cornflakes.

'I was busy asking questions!' he said.

'And not getting any answers!' Beans said. 'The
Mystery Man didn't know who he was, or where he
was, or how he got there, so you're questioning
wasn't much good, was it?'

Beans and James were gloomy because of the
mistake about the footprints the night before.

'Some of us did all right!' I said. Casey's dad had
been very pleased when I'd shown him the page of
my notebook with the bit about the lorry in it. He
was going to follow my information up, because we

knew the Mystery Man hadn't been in the alley beside the cafe when I left the first bin out, but the lorry had been parked outside. Then Casey turned up, the lorry pulled away from the kerb in a big hurry and almost got him, and minutes later I spotted the Mystery Man, when I went out with the second bin.

We'd been able to tell Casey's dad when the Mystery Man was dumped, more or less, because my evidence note about the Casey Crash was timed at 21.53 and we reckoned that we hadn't spent more than five minutes talking about the Balloonograms and eggs, so the dumping must have been done just about 21.48, when the alley was clear.

'If I'd walked out a minute sooner with that bin I'd have been right in the middle of it!' I said.

'Why was he dumped?' said Beans.

'Mugged, probably,' said James. 'He had no I.D. stuff on him. No wallet, no credit cards, not even a letter!'

'We could go and ask questions at the hospital,' I said. 'Maybe something we said would jog his memory. Then we'd be Famous!'

'I don't think they'd let us near him,' said James. 'Someone with amnesia, who's been involved in a mugging . . . that is police work!'

'Here! What's this?' Dad's head poked round the door of the back room. 'What's this balloon doing sticking through my letterbox?'

'Balloon!'

We cleared the room double-quick, into the cafe.

'It's a message!' I gasped.

'It's a ruddy balloon!' Dad said, and he went off grumbling, without waiting for us to explain.

'A message?' said James. 'What sort of message is that?'

'A Bacon Balloonogram!' said Beans. 'Only Casey has to go one better. He's put the Balloonogram in code, and he wants us to figure it out!'

'*Morse!*' said James.

'But Morse is a *sound* code, or a *light* one,' I objected.

'In this case, it is a *write* one,' said Beans. Then we got our copy of the Morse code, which I have in my TSM book, and checked Casey's message against it.

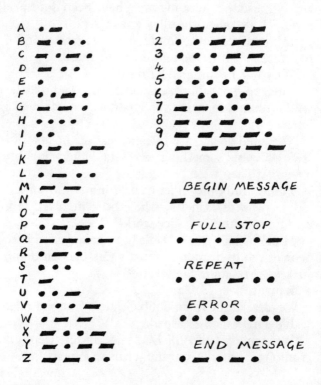

Can you decode the message?

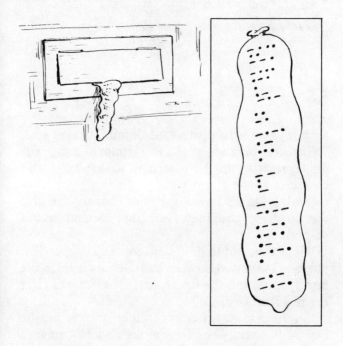

Check the message on the Balloonogram against the Morse code entry in Bodger's TSM book.

Move to **7** when you've got the whole message decoded!

If you need help turn to **11**.

Detective Rating

2 points if you got it right.
Deduct 1 point for each wrong choice.

56

'It *wasn't* to incriminate Paul Gemini!' Casey said. 'Whatever happened about Gemini's alibi, the fingerprints would have seen to it that he wasn't convicted of the crime.'

'So it wasn't a frame-up?' said Beans. 'The idea was to make absolutely sure that Gemini wasn't suspected?'

'He was bound to be suspected,' said Casey. 'But the camera showed the fake Paul Gemini making the fingerprints, and the fingerprint evidence will clear the real Paul Gemini.'

'So the camera is Gemini's Chief Witness for the Defence!' I said. 'The Case of the Candid Camera.'

'The Gemini job was set up in such a way that it clears Paul Gemini of suspicion!' said Casey. 'Gemini was the last man in the cinema, he knew the layout, he knew where the money was kept, he may even have found out the safe combination . . . he was the *obvious* culprit. But the crime was carried out in a very peculiar way . . . a way which *seems* to prove that Paul Gemini, Number One Suspect, absolutely couldn't do it.'

There was a long silence.

'And as far as you are concerned the *fact* that the

facts show he *couldn't* have done it points to Paul Gemini being the guilty man!' said James. 'It is obvious, isn't it . . . to anyone like Superbrain here! Gemini *couldn't* have committed the crime . . . therefore he must have done it!'

Casey went red! I thought he was going to knock James's head off. James shouldn't have said it the way he did. James and Casey are great when they work together on a case, but most of the time they are competing with each other to see who is the best detective. It gets dead boring sometimes, when you have to listen to it.

'I don't think we can prove anything from the way the case was set up,' I said.

'Only that it isn't a straightforward job,' said Casey. 'There must be a reason for that, and I reckon it is to do with Paul Gemini and his one-hundred-per-cent alibi!'

'But you can't prove it,' said James.

'No,' said Casey. 'I can't. You know I can't. This is a Not Proven case all the way . . . '

'The evidence proves one thing to me,' said Beans, suddenly.

'What?'

'It proves that this case isn't a Who-dunnit. It's a How-was-it-done! If we can work that out, then we'll probably know Who-dunnit!'

'Right!' said Casey. 'I reckon Paul Gemini did the safe job . . . so the question is how could he do it, and have a one-hundred-per-cent alibi at the same time?'

'He *could* do it—if the crime *didn't happen at the time it was supposed to*!' Beans said.

'Eh?'

'If the money was stolen before 21.30!' Beans said. 'Before the *real* Paul Gemini left the Star Cinema.'

'The money would be there,' said Casey. 'The second feature began at . . . when?'

'20.15,' I said, flipping open my notebook to show the details Casey had given us.

'No-one would go into a cinema halfway through the last show,' said Casey. 'The ticket booth closes, the money is taken up to the Manager's office . . . '

'Smithson says he put the money in the safe at 22.25!' James objected.

'Supposing the money was *already gone* by then?' Casey said. 'Suppose Smithson is lying?'

'He might be lying, but the camera isn't!' James said. 'The camera shows the fake Paul Gemini working at the safe at 22.35!'

Then I did one of my brilliant bits!

'Clocks!' I said.

'What?'

'Suppose Smithson and the real Paul Gemini are in it together. They altered the time on the clock!'

'I get you,' Casey said, slowly. 'They altered the time, switched on the camera, staged a nice little scene and then Paul Gemini cleared off to set up his alibi! There is no fake Paul Gemini.'

'Fingerprints?' said James, suddenly. 'How did they work the fingerprints?'

'Easy!' I said. 'I bet Smithson called Burn or Roy or Mrs Patrick up to the office about something. I bet he got one of them to leave *their* fingerprints where the camera had shown Paul Gemini leaving his . . . '

'After the *real* fingerprints had been carefully removed!' said Casey.

'So Smithson and the real Paul Gemini staged the whole thing between them, giving Gemini a cast iron alibi, and making sure that *no-one* else could be blamed, because of the evidence of the camera . . . '

'Doesn't work!' said Beans, suddenly. 'You've forgotten something!'

What have the squad forgotten?

Is it . . .

That Mrs Patrick left at 21.30? Turn to **2**.

That the second feature didn't end until 22.15? Turn to **9**.

That Smithson says he left the cinema at 22.30? Turn to **16**.

That Derek Burn and Harry Roy departed at 22.25? Turn to **24**.

That Paul Gemini was discovered in the alley at 21.50 approx? Turn to **28**.

That someone drove the lorry? Turn to **38**.

That someone returned the lorry to the scrap yard? Turn to **41**.

That someone unloaded the Mini from the lorry? Turn to **53**.

That Bodger bumped into Paul Gemini? Turn to **59**.

That Smithson says Paul Gemini brought him plaice and chips shortly after 22.00? Turn to **66**.

That Paul Gemini was taken straight to hospital from the alley? Turn to **72**.

If you need a clue, turn to **79**.

Detective Rating

1 point for each correct chip shop!
0 points for any you got wrong.

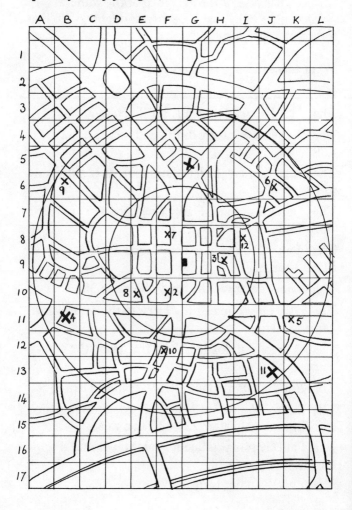

57

It was dead easy, really. I went to Bird's, the Titanic and El Munchoe, but I didn't get any free suppers.

'The whole thing is a cold chip!' Beans said, when we gathered back at the garage. Nobody had got any clues, but some chip shops weren't helpful about giving information, so it didn't prove anything.

'What do we now?' James asked. 'Leave it to the police?'

Nobody liked that idea. It was our case. Somebody had tried to frame Paul Gemini, and knocked him on the head to do it. We reckoned we could find out who it was and show Casey's dad we weren't just silly kids who made mistakes about protecting footprints from the rain and asked daft questions.

'The Mystery Squad never gives up on a case!' I said.

'Never giving up is all right, but where do we start? We can't interview Paul Gemini at the hospital . . . '

'No fear!' said Casey, quickly. 'Dad would never let us.'

'We can't go accusing Smithson of lying, because we don't know what he said about the chips, and anyway the police won't want us nosing around the Star Cinema putting witnesses on their guard . . . '

'That's it!' said Casey, snapping his fingers.

'What?'

'The one place we *can* go. The one thing we *can* investigate. The Omega scrap yard, and the get-away lorry! Maybe we'll turn something up there . . . '

'Like what?' said James, not very hopefully.

'Like a rather large missing detail,' said Casey. 'Bodger, have you got that photo Dad brought in on your files?'

I had to rummage about a bit for it, but I got it. Somebody must have been at my file box with mucky fingers. It wasn't my chocolate, but the picture was a bit smeared.

'Eugh!' said Casey, holding it out in front of him. 'Just what I thought. Something that was there last night was missing when this photograph was taken this morning. It just could be important!'

What's missing from the lorry?

If you need to refresh your memory, look at the picture of the lorry in **70**.

If you know, turn to **15**.

If you need help, turn to **17**.

58

That's your clue!
Go to **55** when you've worked it out!

59

Right! Work out why, and turn to **6**.

60

Yes, but not quite . . . go to **3** and think again!

61

Wrong. There is no hurry to photograph the bins.
They won't run away. Turn to **26** and think again.

62

3+rd   = *third*

 = *house*

= bone−B=one−e=*on*
−B   −E

−L = light−L+R=*right*
+R

THIRD HOUSE ON RIGHT is the third line.
Go to **12**.

Detective Rating

If you decided straight away to walk *back to Casey's together, score 4 points.*

Deduct 1 point for each wrong choice you made!

You score 2 bonus points if you worked out why, *first time!*

63

We walked back to Casey's, doing all we could to look as ordinary as possible, and sticking tight together in case somebody tried to jump us. We reckoned we'd be safe that way, and we might then spot the person who was after us. Anyway, we'd get a chance to contact Casey's dad.

It was a real let-down!

Nobody came after us.

I'd been going to bash the somebody with my Dreaded Bodgeroon Bumper Bash, but in the end I didn't get to do it.

Casey's dad wasn't at home, so Casey locked the door and posted us all as look-outs, then he went to telephone the police station.

I was crouching by the window, and then I *saw* someone . . .

Who did Bodger spot?

If you think it is . . .

The *real* Paul Gemini? Turn to **78**.

The fake Paul Gemini? Turn to **74**.

Fat, bald Harry Roy? Turn to **36**.

Casey's dad? Turn to **31**.

Somebody else? Turn to **22**.

Mr Smithson? Turn to **10**.

Detective Rating

2 points if you realised that sooner or later Gemini Number Two would have to use the toilet!

1 point if you needed a clue.

64

This is what happened:

We ended up celebrating in our cafe, at Casey's dad's expense.

We had sausage, beans and chips, double, and lots of Coke, and free tickets from Mr Smithson at the Star Cinema for all four of us.

'What's on?' I demanded, and Beans wrote it out in the window for us, with her finger.

'Oh no! groaned James. 'Not that!'

'Brilliant!' I said, and it was.

Decode this one . . . no points!

Now turn to the Detective Rating Chart on p 96 to find out how good a detective you are.

P.S. if you can't decode it, turn to **84**.

65

If you make a run for it, the person watching you will know *you* know that you are being watched. You lose your advantage, and will perhaps scare the watcher away . . . then he or she will avoid capture. Go to **25** and think again.

66

Irrelevant! Turn to **56** and think again.

67

Casey took great care not to disturb the scene of the crime . . . he isn't a detective's son for nothing! Turn to **14** and think again.

68

Right . . . but why the hurry? If you know turn to **14** . If you need help turn to **71**.

69

= watch+ing=*watching*

U = *you*

= hook−H+L=*look*

= hat−H=*at*

WATCHING YOU LOOK AT is the second line. Go to **12**.

Detective Rating

If you spotted the time factor, take 3 points.
Deduct 1 point for each clue you needed.

70

'The digital clock in the picture is showing 22.35,'
James said. 'At 22.35 our Mystery Man was being
lifted on to a stretcher, to be taken off to hospital! He
was in *our* house, with us, and several policemen!'

'Not a bad alibi!' Casey added, with a grin.

'He *fixed* the clock!' I said.

'Good thinking, Bodge, but it's no go,' said Casey.
'The Star Cinema closed last night at 22.20. The
Manager left at 22.30, after locking up the takings in
his safe. He left one of the ushers, Paul Gemini, to
close the place up for him. Gemini apparently waited
until the Manager had left, and then went coolly up
to the office and helped himself!'

'Arrest Paul Gemini!' I said.

'Our Mystery Man got his memory back this
morning, after the shock had worn off. He *is* Paul
Gemini!'

I grabbed the photograph.

'But that *is* him!' I said. 'I know it is! I
mean . . . look! It *has* to be!'

'Or somebody carefully *disguised* as Paul Gemini,'
said James, slowly. 'Somebody who planned exactly
what he was doing. He had to get hold of the *real* Paul
Gemini somehow . . . '

'Gemini goes out for fish and chips each night, about 21.30,' said Casey. 'The Manager of the Star Cinema, Mr Smithson, confirms that he went last night, because Smithson had ordered cod, and Gemini got him plaice. They had a row about it.'

'He got plaice because he didn't *know* what to get Smithson!' I burst in. 'The man who went to the fish and chip shop didn't know, because he wasn't the *same* Paul Gemini who left the Star Cinema, right?'

'Exactly,' said Casey. 'The way my dad sees it, somebody was waiting for Gemini when he came out of the cinema, bonked him over the head, dumped him, using the lorry, and drove straight back to the cinema where he went in, disguised as Paul Gemini and carried on with his job as usual, until the Manager left at 22.30. Then the fake Paul Gemini went up to the office, and removed the takings!'

'How did he manage to fool the people at the cinema?' said Beans. 'He must have been a great actor.'

'He'd be in the dark most of the time . . . ' Casey said.

'And wearing a uniform,' said James. 'It's like a postman, or a policeman . . . most people notice the uniform, not the face.'

'The Cinema patrons would do that, but not the staff!' Beans objected. 'He wouldn't be just a face to them, he'd be a person!'

'Mrs Patrick at the cash desk goes off work at 21.45, when they've counted the takings. Gemini was away from the cinema then, and she wasn't around to see the fake Gemini who came back.'

'Other ushers?' asked James.

'There are two. Harry Roy and Derek Burn. I've got their pictures from Dad as well as Smithson's. Roy and Burn were busy. They saw Gemini, but they weren't talking to him,' Casey said.

Roy

Burn

Smithson

Mrs Patrick

'The Manager talked to him,' said Beans. 'You said they had a row about the fish . . . getting plaice instead of cod. Right?'

'Right,' said Casey. 'Mr Smithson remembers it well . . . and he *is*, or *was*, prepared to swear that he talked to Paul Gemini between 22.00 and 22.15 last night, when they were locking up.'

'When the *real* Paul Gemini was in our house,' I said.

'It must have been a brilliant disguise,' said Beans, enviously. 'Imagine standing there with the Manager for over a quarter of an hour, and not being spotted!'

'There's the red hair, of course,' said Casey. 'Paul Gemini has red hair. If the fake one had a red wig that might go a long way to convincing people that he was who he claimed to be.'

'Eyes!' said James.

'What?'

'I wonder if Casey's dad has checked up on Smithson's eyesight,' said James. 'Suppose he can't see well, but he is too vain to wear glasses? That might account for his failing to spot that it wasn't the real Paul Gemini he was talking to.'

'The fake Paul Gemini would have to know that,' said Casey.

'As far as I can see the fake Paul Gemini had a lot of inside information,' said James. 'He had to know a lot about Gemini in the first place, to be able to prepare a disguise nobody could see through. He had to know where the money was kept, and how the safe could be broken into. He had to know what time the real Gemini went out each night for the fish and chips . . . he did go every night, didn't he?'

'Yep. Every night,' said Casey.

'Not to our shop!' said Beans.

'Our shop is at least fifteen minutes away from the Star Cinema,' I said. 'There are others in between. Shops that stay open longer than we do.'

'Very tight schedule!' said James. 'We ought to think about that.'

We worked out the timings on the Gemini job as closely as we could, from Casey's information and my notes.

THE GEMINI JOB

<u>Timings</u>:

18.00 - Staff arrive Star Cinema. Gemini among first to arrive.

18.30 - Star Cinema opens.

18.45 - First feature.

20.10 - Brief interlude. Gemini on duty at kiosk.

20.15 - Second feature.

21.30 approx. - Gemini attacked and knocked unconcious.

21.45 - Mrs. Patrick leaves cinema.

21.50 approx. - Gemini dumped in alley.

22.00 - Fake Paul Gemini returns to cinema.

22.15 - Second feature finishes.

22.25 - Remaining staff Roy Burn depart. Smithson puts money in safe.

22.30 - Smithson leaves. Fake Gemini is still locking up.

22.35 - Fake Gemini robs safe.

22.40 - Gemini is removed in ambulance.

'When did the fake Gemini get the chips?' Beans asked. 'If it's twenty minutes from the Star to here . . . '

'Ten, if he broke the rules,' said Casey. 'And the way he buzzed off from here suggests he didn't bother much with the Highway Code.'

'We know the lorry left here at 21.50 or just about then,' I said. 'We're all witnesses to that. Whoever dumped Gemini had to be back at the Star Cinema by 22.00! Doesn't leave much time for getting chips.'

'Unless the chips were brought much earlier than that,' said Beans.

That was when Casey's dad walked in.

'Casey?' he said. 'That your lorry?' and he tossed a photograph down on the old crate we use instead of a table.

'OBJ 393Y,' said Casey. 'That's it Dad! Where did it turn up?'

'Omega Scrap,' said Casey's dad, making it sound as if Casey had asked a silly question. 'Where else?'

I didn't want Casey's dad to think we were all silly, so I thought I'd ask a brilliant question that would show him how we were busy solving the case.

'I've got a question, Mr Peters,' I said.

'Yes, young Bodger?' he said, with a sigh.

'What I want to know is: *Were the chips cold?*'

'Chips?' he snapped.

'Mr Smithson's chips,' I said. 'The chips with the plai . . . '

The door banged behind Casey's dad.

'Oh Bodge!' groaned James.

'Punkhead!' said Beans.

'It was a *serious* question,' I said. 'I mean, I think it's really very important.'

'Only to the son of a chip shop owner!' said Casey.

'It is important,' I insisted. 'We know the person driving the lorry hadn't time to buy fish and chips *and* get back to the Star Cinema by ten o'clock. So if the fish and chips were hot when they got to Mr Smithson there *must* have been a second person in it. The fake Paul Gemini and someone else who drove the lorry.'

'He's right!' James said.

'Yes,' said Casey, slowly. 'Yes, he is. Partly, anyway. There is another way to read that clue . . . Suppose that the man who dumped Paul Gemini also delivered the chips, dressed up as Paul. If that is the case and Mr Smithson says the chips were *hot*, then it proves that . . . '

What does it prove?

If you think it proves . . .

That the *real* Paul Gemini bought the chips before he was knocked out, turn to **23**.

That Harry Roy or Derek Burn must have bought the chips turn to **5**.

That Mr Smithson is lying about the chips, turn to **35**.

That the man in the lorry bought the chips *before* he pounced on Paul Gemini, turn to **29**.

71

You're really wet if you can't get this one! What is causing the ripples? Go to **14** when you've figured out what that has to do with taking the photograph quickly!

72

Nothing to do with it! Turn to **56** and think again.

73

Right, but not *exactly* . . . go to **3** and think again.

74

Pie in your eye! Go to **63** and try again.

75

Casey photographed the footprints first because they were in danger from the rain, but he took lots of other photographs (see picture in **14**). Go to **14** and try again.

Detective Rating

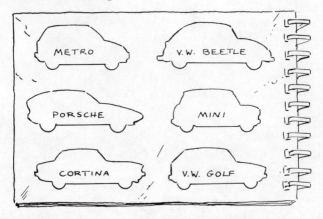

2 points if you got it without looking at the pictures in 1.
1 point if you had to look.

76

We went on an Austin Mini Hunt to the Omega scrap yard. The man at the gate thought we were just kids, and let us nose around. We thought we'd find the car easily.

'Where is it?' Beans said.

'Don't know,' said James.

'We'd better start looking,' said Casey, grimly.

We started checking the cars.

There were trillions of them!
'Which one is it?' Beans said.

Can you find the missing Mini?

Go to **45** if you think you've got it.

If you need a clue, turn to **37**.

Detective Rating

2 points for spotting Beans!
0 points for the custard-pied!

77

'Beans!' I hissed. 'Nip in through the window, quickly!'

'Why?' she said, looking at me as if I was mad.

'Because there's a man following us . . . ' I said.

'No there isn't!' she said.

'Your note said there was!'

'My note said someone was watching you. Someone was. And I was watching him! He didn't come after you! He went straight into the scrap yard and headed for the Mini.'

'And?'

'And I don't know,' said Beans. 'I may be daft, but I'm not that daft. I wasn't going to follow Paul Gemini into the scrap yard on my own, no fear!'

'Gemini?' James and Casey had joined us.

'I *think* he went to the Mini,' said Beans. 'I decided it was too dangerous to go in after him so I just hung about outside waiting for him to re-appear and . . . '

'And what?' said James, impatiently.

'And he *didn't*,' said Beans.

'Still in there?' said Casey.

'I don't think so,' said Beans. 'I climbed a tree, after I'd been waiting a bit. I could see into the scrap yard from there, and I could see the Mini, but I couldn't see Gemini . . . '

'Lots of entrances,' said James.

'I reckon you are a fink, Beans,' I said. 'If it had been the Mighty Bodger Bacon I'd have captured him removing the loot from the Mini and we would all have been heroes for solving the Gemini Job.'

'Oh no you wouldn't,' said James. 'You'd probably have got your head bashed in.'

'That is just kid's stuff, Bodge,' said Casey. 'Beans was absolutely and completely right *not* to go barging in on her own after a suspect . . . '

'Very sensible,' agreed James.

'I usually am,' said Beans.

'CASEY? CASEY?' Casey's dad's voice boomed. We opened the door.

He came in, looking none too pleased. 'What's all this about then, Casey?' he said.

'The loot was hidden in a Mini in the scrap yard and Paul Gemini has just been in to get it!' I said. 'Beans spotted him. If it had been me I would have . . . '

'Gemini!' said Casey's dad. 'Gemini did *what*?'

'He took something from an old Mini in the scrap

yard a few minutes ago, Dad,' said Casey. 'We think it might have been the loot. We didn't touch the Mini in case . . . '

'*Casey!*' groaned his father.

'Beans *saw* Gemini, Dad,' said Casey.

'At 12.31 exactly,' said Beans. 'I noted the time, so Bodge could put it in his TSM notebook.'

'At 12.31, eh?' said Casey's dad. 'That's interesting. Now let *me* tell *you* something. At 10.00 this morning Paul Gemini was released from the General Hospital and brought to my office, where he has been from approximately 10.35 this morning, until I left him five minutes ago. We're going through mug-shots to see if any of them stir his somewhat hazy memory.'

'Gemini was with you?' Beans goggled at him.

'Right!' said Casey's dad. 'In my office, with me, where I'm going, right now! And I don't want to hear a squeak from you lot again. See? I've had enough of your muck-ups!'

Off he went.

'I *saw* Gemini,' said Beans. 'I know I did.'

'So did I, remember?' I said.

'Did he recognise you?' Casey asked.

'No, but . . . '

'We must both have seen the *fake* Paul Gemini,' said Beans.

'Still dressed up in his fancy dress?' James said.

We were absolutely baffled.

Beans and I had *seen* Paul Gemini . . . but we couldn't have, because he was with Mr Peters at the police station at the time.

'Another unbeatable alibi!' said James.

'Let's go over it all again,' Casey said, and we did, until we got to the photograph taken in Mr Smithson's office, the one of the fake Gemini working at the safe.

'Hold it!' said Casey. 'Something wrong here. This seems to be a highly professional job, right? Well, if it is . . . there's something odd about the fake Paul Gemini's safe-breaking technique!'

What is it?

Check the picture in 7.

If you know what Casey is on about, turn to 40.

If you need a clue turn to 32.

78

Custard pied! Go to **63** and try again!

79

No-one can be in two places at the same time! Look for someone who was! That is your clue. Go to **56** and think again.

80

Wrong. The man has already been moved! Go to **26** and think again.

81

It certainly does that, but . . . go to **3** and think again.

82

Wrong! Go to **1** and try again.

83

Flush the answer out, then turn to **64**!

84

Your very last custard pie—but no lost points!

3^{-R}_{-E} = three − R = thee − E = *The*

= *Case*

= *Book*

10^{-I}_{+F} = *Of*

= *Sherlock Holmes.*

= THE CASE BOOK OF SHERLOCK HOLMES.

The Mystery Squad Detective Rating

This chart will show you the Detective Rating you've earned by completing this Solve it Yourself Mystery.

You should be able to improve your score as you tackle further mysteries in the series and pick up more tips from them. Keep a note of your scores for future reference.

Your Score	Detective Rating
60–70	Sherlock Holmes!
50–59	Super Sleuth!
40–49	Ace Detective
30–39	Detective—1st Class
20–29	Detective—2nd Class
11–19	Junior Detective
6–10	Trainee
0–5	Beginner

If you've enjoyed reading this Solve it Yourself Mystery and would like to test your detective skills further, here are some more titles in the same series:

The Mystery Squad and the Dead Man's Message
The Mystery Squad and the Artful Dodger
The Mystery Squad and Mr Midnight
The Mystery Squad and the Whistling Teeth
The Mystery Squad and the Creeping Castle